Disney

FROZEN

Illustrated by GRACE LEE,

MASSIMILIANO NARCISO, and

ANDREA CAGOL

Written by VICTORIA SA[...]

Designed by TONY FEJERAN

A GOLDEN BOOK • NEW YORK

randomhousekids.com
ISBN 978-0-7364-3471-3 (trade) — ISBN 978-0-7364-3472-0 (ebook)
Printed in the United States of America
30 29 28 27 26 25 24 23 22

Not long ago in the kingdom of ARENDELLE, summer had arrived!

But it was winter inside the castle where
Princesses ELSA and ANNA were playing. Elsa
had **magical powers** and could create things
out of snow and ice! She made a snowman
named Olaf. Anna was delighted.

Then Elsa accidentally hurt Anna.

The king and queen rushed both girls
to the mystical trolls in the mountains.

The trolls cured Anna by **CHANGING HER MEMORIES** of Elsa's magic. They cautioned that others would fear Elsa's power. To help her control it, Elsa's parents gave her gloves.

With the castle gates closed, Elsa stayed away from Anna—she never wanted to hurt her again. But

Elsa missed
ANNA.

Anna
missed
ELSA.

Years later, the king and queen were lost at sea. Without their parents, both princesses grew **LONELIER** and **LONELIER**.

Soon it was time for Elsa to take over as QUEEN. She was terrified that without her gloves, she might lose control of her powers in front of everyone!

Anna, on the other hand, was excited to meet new people—especially a prince named Hans.

THEY FELL IN LOVE!

Elsa gathered all her courage to take off her
gloves—and was successfully crowned Queen
of Arendelle!

With her gloves back on, Elsa proudly stood before her people.

But when Anna told Elsa that she wanted to marry Hans, Elsa forbade it. How could Anna want to marry a man she had only just met?

Frustrated, Anna tried to stop her sister and accidentally **PULLED OFF** one glove.

Without her glove and upset with
Anna, Elsa accidentally **exposed** her
secret powers. Ice and snow blasted
from her hand, covering the kingdom.

Fearing she might hurt
someone and ruin her
kingdom,
ELSA FLED.

Anna thought it was her fault Elsa's powers had been revealed. She rushed off to find her sister.

She hired a mountain man named Kristoff to be her guide.

In time, Anna and Kristoff found a snowman named Olaf. He was alive!

Anna **REMEMBERED** him—and the good times she had shared with her sister. Olaf led the way to Elsa.

Elsa was enjoying her time alone.

Now she was free to create whatever she wanted.

She built an ICE PALACE.

Anna begged Elsa to go home
to thaw her frozen kingdom.
   But Elsa feared she couldn't
control her powers.

Angry and afraid, Elsa accidentally cast a
magic **freezing spell** on her little sister . . .

. . . and then created a **GIANT SNOWMAN.**
Anna and Kristoff ran. Olaf ran, too!

Anna's hair began to turn white. Kristoff led her to the trolls for help.

The trolls advised, "Only an act of TRUE LOVE can thaw a frozen heart."

Anna needed Hans for a true love's kiss!

Quickly, Kristoff and Anna headed back to Arendelle.

When Anna found Hans, he **REFUSED** to kiss her. His plan all along had been to take over the kingdom. Anna was crushed!

Anna realized that Kristoff loved her! She needed all her strength to find him.

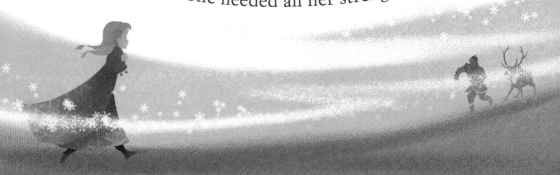

Meanwhile, Elsa had returned to Arendelle to save her kingdom. But now she was in **TERRIBLE DANGER**.

When Anna saw Hans, she knew what she had to do.

Anna
SAVED
Elsa.

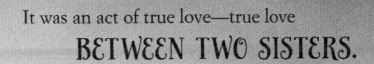

It was an act of true love—true love
BETWEEN TWO SISTERS.

Soon the ice melted. And Anna realized she was in love with Kristoff. As for Elsa, she became queen again—a good queen who had learned from her sister that **LOVE** was the key to controlling her powers.